JAMES THE *Christmas* GROUCH

USA TODAY BESTSELLING AUTHOR

IVY SMOAK

This book is a work of fiction. Names, characters, places, and incidents are fictitious. Any resemblance to actual persons, living or dead, events, or locales is purely coincidental.

ISBN: 9798764064888

2021 First Edition

Chapter 1

3 DAYS BEFORE CHRISTMAS

"That one," I said and pointed at a tree across the lot. I grabbed James' hand and pulled him toward it. He didn't say a word as I dropped his hand and walked around the tree, examining it. The branches were so symmetrical it almost didn't look real. I took a step back and stared up at the beautiful evergreen. "It's perfect." When James didn't say anything I turned toward him. "Don't you think?"

"If you think it's perfect, then so do I."

I pressed my lips together. "James, I want us to choose a tree together. That's the whole point." I slid my hand back into his.

He smiled. "I want to give you the best Christmas you've ever had. And if you think this tree is perfect, we should get this one." He ran his fingers through my hair.

He always said the right things. But I didn't want him to just say the right things. I wanted him to have the best Christmas ever too. "Well, let's keep looking. Just to make sure it's the right one."

I tucked myself into his side as we started walking around the Christmas tree lot again. The night air was chilly, but I always felt warm when I was beside him. I smiled as he wrapped his arm tighter around me. How many times had I dreamt about this? Getting to love someone at Christmas? It was like all my childhood dreams coming true. All my wishes to Santa.

I let him lead the way this time, taking it all in. This was our first Christmas together. I didn't want to force all of my traditions on him. He said he had grown up with a fake tree. For some reason that made me sad. But maybe that's what he wanted. I was just about to tell him we could go to a department store and buy one when he stopped in front of a tree that was slightly lopsided.

"What about this one?" he asked. "I feel like it could use a good home."

I couldn't help the grin that spread across my face. The tree really did need a home. If we didn't take it, I wasn't sure anyone else would. I looked up at him. "I love this one."

"Yeah?"

I nodded. "So much better than that other stupid one."

James stared at me skeptically.

"Really. This one is so us."

He laughed. "I'm not really sure what you mean by that. It's a little crooked, isn't it? I was kinda joking when I said we should get it."

I bumped him with my hip. "It's not crooked. It's perfectly...imperfect."

He smiled. "Hmm. Perfectly imperfect. I like that." He kissed the side of my forehead. "So what next?" He bent down to study the trunk. "Do we take it up to the checkout?"

"As much as I'd like to watch you figure out how to do that, no. We just tell the guy at the front that we want this one. Come on." I grabbed his hand and pulled him through the trees until we found someone to help us.

"You're ridiculously cute," James said as we watched the tree guy give the trunk a fresh cut.

I scrunched my nose up. *I knew I should have worn heels.* He never said I looked cute when I wore heels. I looked down at my flat boots. This Christmas wasn't supposed to be cute. If anything, it should be sexy. Tons of mistletoe. And roaring fires to snuggle in front of. My traditions seemed childish.

"What's wrong with cute?" he asked, reading the expression on my face.

It was weird that he could do that. Or maybe that wasn't the strange part. Maybe it was just odd that I now had someone in my life that cared about the expression on my face. The thought made me smile. "Nothing's wrong with cute. It's just that I want our new Christmas traditions together to be a little more naughty than nice."

"Then you're wearing a few too many layers."

I laughed and hit his arm as the tree guy finished tying the tree down to the roof. "Just wait until we start decorating." I started walking away from James backwards and gave him an exaggerated wink.

He smiled and caught up to me. "Maybe Santa's granting me my wish a little early."

"If you're wishing for me naked, that's a ridiculous wish. You were going to get that either way."

"It's definitely going to be the best Christmas ever then." He beat me to the door and opened it up for me.

For some reason we always ended up racing to the car. He liked opening up the door for me and I still wasn't used to having someone open the door for me. Dating him was an adjustment. The best kind of adjustment.

"Thank you," I smiled and kissed the tip of his nose before sliding into the passenger's seat.

He quickly climbed into his side and started the ignition.

I pulled my feet up onto the seat and stared at him as he shifted the car into drive.

"What?" he asked with a smile.

"Nothing, it's just that I never really see you drive anymore. Are you sure we need a driver? I mean, the subway..."

"Penny, we've talked about this. You don't have to take the subway."

"I know I don't have to. But I can. Ian has to go out of his way to drop me off. And with the new offices you're setting up, he's going to have to drive you in the morning. I don't want to be a bother."

I turned away from him and looked out at the city streets. I could just make out the huge Rockefeller tree in the distance. It was beautiful. Truly it was the most beautiful part of Christmastime in New York City. I was still holding out on snow being beautiful here too though. I had a feeling a snowfall would be the calmness that this city so drastically needed.

"Penny, you are never a bother." He placed his hand on my knee. "And for the millionth time, it's Ian's job to drive us around. He doesn't mind."

"Technically it's his job to drive *you* around. Not me."

"Penny, you're my fiancée."

"Your point?"

He laughed. "My point is that what's mine is yours."

It wasn't the first time we'd had this conversation. The problem was that I didn't need everything he was offering. I wasn't used to the extravagantness of his life. Sometimes I craved normalcy. A ride in the subway once a day didn't seem like such a bad thing to me.

He let his hand fall from my knee.

My body instantly felt cold. How could his hands do that? Warm me when I didn't even realize I needed warming? I didn't want to fight with him. "Okay. If you're sure Ian doesn't mind."

The corners of his mouth turned up. "He doesn't mind. Ask him yourself next time you see him. You know, when you stop randomly giving him time off."

"James! It's only a few days till Christmas. He deserved time off tonight. And we didn't need his help getting a tree. It's supposed to be a special thing, just the two of us."

"Well that might be a problem," James said as he pulled into the parking lot beneath our apartment building.

Rob was standing by the elevator examining the slot where you had to insert a keycard.

"I didn't know Rob was coming," I said.

"Well, he mentioned he was coming to town for Christmas. But I didn't know he was coming over tonight."

"Oh. I thought your parents weren't doing anything this year."

"About that." James unbuckled his seatbelt. "Penny..." his voice trailed off as Rob pounded his hand against the window of the passenger's side.

"It's freezing, guys. Let me up." He crossed his arms around himself.

I laughed and stepped out of the car. "Of course you're cold. Where is your coat?" He was only wearing a sweater.

"It's warmer in Delaware. Give me a hug to warm me up, you dirty temptress." He wrapped his arms around me.

I laughed. "It's only a little more than two hours from here, Rob. I doubt it's any warmer there."

"I swear it is." He kissed my cheek. "It's good to see you, Penny."

I smiled up at him. "You too."

"It's good you're here," James said. "Because I have no idea what to do with this." He gestured to the tree.

Rob laughed and pulled James' scarf off and twirled it around his own neck. "Your knight in shining armor is here, my lady," he said and winked at me.

James exhaled loudly. I would never tire of seeing the way that Rob pushed James' buttons.

"Here, catch," Rob said as he pulled a pocketknife from his back pocket and tossed it at James. "The woman and I will go start a fire."

"Oh, no, Rob, take my key. I was going to help him with the tree." My romantic evening was suddenly fluttering away with the wind that was picking up.

"I got it, baby," James said. "Go get him warm before he catches pneumonia." He nodded toward Rob who was still shivering despite the scarf.

"Are you sure?"

"Yup, I've got this." He turned back to the car and started fidgeting with the rope.

I followed Rob over to the elevator. As the doors closed I saw James scratching the scruff on his chin and examining the tree on the roof of his car. I smiled, knowing that he had probably sent me away because he had no idea what he was doing. He still wasn't good at showing me every side of him.

"Thanks for letting me stay with you guys," Rob said.

"Are you staying with us?"

He laughed. "Of course. Where do you expect me to stay? My parents'?" He seemed to shiver worse at that idea.

"No, I guess not." Whenever Rob visited, he always crashed at our place. I loved having him in town, I did. But he didn't really fit into my naughty Christmas. I was hoping to snuggle up to James in front of the fire. Not set Rob in front of it and hope he didn't catch a cold.

"What's bothering you, Penny?"

I laughed. Apparently all the Hunter men could read me now. "Nothing." I stepped off the elevator and unlocked the door to our apartment.

"You're not getting off that easy, sweet cheeks."

I set my keys down on the kitchen counter. What was bothering me? It wasn't that Rob was here. I loved when he visited. I looked around the apartment. There wasn't a single Christmas decoration in place. Growing up, my mom would always decorate the day after Thanksgiving. Our house would resemble a Christmas themed store. And I loved it. I loved the holiday spirit. I loved how it brought us all together.

But James was busy starting his new company. And I had been busy studying for finals. It was three days before Christmas and we had only just gotten a tree. I bit the inside of my lip. This wasn't what I expected. For some reason, I just assumed everything would be the same. But of course it wasn't. I wasn't even living in the same state. For the first time ever, I wasn't going to be with my parents on Christmas Eve or Christmas morning. I was trying to be good about the changes. But I had never really been great at change. And it was off-putting that it looked like a Grinch lived in our apartment.

"Earth to Penny." Rob waved his hand in front of my face.

I turned toward him. "Does James hate Christmas?"

He laughed. "Hate Christmas? What kind of monster hates Christmas?"

"I don't know, but look around." I gestured to the living room. "I had to drag him out tonight to get a tree. We haven't decorated at all."

"Oh. That. He's just not used to decorating. My parents' staff always did that."

"But he hasn't been living at home for years."

Rob shrugged as he opened up the fridge door and pulled out a beer. "Want one?"

I shook my head as I walked farther into the kitchen. "No, that's okay." I pulled out a pot, poured some milk in it, and turned on the stove. Hot chocolate could fix anything. Maybe it could even trick James into liking Christmas.

Rob popped off the cap of his beer. "I'm a little surprised Ellen didn't decorate for him."

"She offered almost as much as I did. But he was really dismissive about it. He hates Christmas, doesn't he?" It felt like my heart was beating faster as I waited for him to respond.

"He always liked it growing up. I don't know what to tell you."

God. I was over-thinking it. I was over-thinking everything. "But it's not just that, Rob. I know he's getting me the world's greatest gift. And I have no idea what to get him." I grabbed a mug out of the cupboard.

"Head."

I almost dropped the cup, but caught it before it smashed against the granite. "That's not what I'm talking about," I hissed as I gently placed it against the counter.

He smiled. "Well, I'm telling you. He just wants head."

"That's not..." I sighed and leaned against the counter. "That isn't even a gift."

Rob put his hands against his chest. "I knew you were the woman of my dreams. If you're just handing out blowjobs, I'll take one."

I hit his arm. "Stop, Rob. I'm being serious. What do I get him?" I grabbed two more mugs out of the cupboard and pulled out the cocoa mix.

"And I'm being serious. Every guy wants head as a present. Always. It's literally always the answer."

I shook my head. Rob was so freaking unhelpful. "Is there something that he's always wanted?"

"Head."

"Not helping." I pulled the hot milk off the stove and poured it into the cups. I had just started to mix the cocoa in when James stumbled into the apartment with the tree over his shoulder.

The mixture of freshly cut pine and hot chocolate made any sense of our apartment being un-Christmassy evaporate.

Rob put down his beer, lifted up his hot cocoa, and blew on it. He started walking past James, not offering any help with the tree. "Penny wants to know why you hate Christmas, Mr. Grinch." He slapped him on the stomach with his free hand and then collapsed on the couch.

Rob. "I didn't...that wasn't..." my voice trailed off. Because I did. And it was. I cringed.

James set the tree down in the foyer and ran his hand through his hair. "I don't hate Christmas, Penny."

"I know." I rushed over to him with the cups of cocoa. *I think I know.* I offered him one of the cups, hoping it would distract him. I wanted to sing carols and decorate the Christmas tree. I didn't want to talk about the past. Even if he did hate Christmas, I could make him like it. I knew I could. I just needed time.

He brushed off his hands on his wool coat and grabbed a cup. "I don't hate Christmas," he repeated. The mug effectively disappeared beneath his big hands.

"Look around, man," Rob said from the other room. "Where's all the Christmas garland? And stockings? And strings of lights?"

Not helping, Rob!

James gave me a smile, but it didn't quite reach his eyes. "I'm sorry that I've been so busy, Penny. I know getting Hunter Tech off the ground is taking up a lot of my time, but..."

"James it's okay. All I wanted was the tree. And now we have the tree." I looked down at the beautiful, lopsided tree. "Oh, shit."

"What?" He looked up from his mug.

"I forgot about the tree stand. We can't put it up without a tree stand."

James looked down at his watch. "I'm not sure what stores will still be open. Maybe Ellen has..."

"We're not calling Ellen about this." I loved Ellen. I loved Ian. But I wasn't used to having help. And every time James asked them for something it made me feel like I was letting him down. How had I forgotten about the tree stand?

"The game is on!" Rob shouted from the other room.

"I'll pick one up in the morning, okay?" I said. "And then when you get home tomorrow we can set it up. Just the two of us."

"That sounds perfect."

We walked together into the living room and joined Rob on the couch. He had already kicked off his shoes and made himself at home.

"Everyone's already talking about New York's hottest couple heating up the freezing cold city." Rob flashed us a picture on his phone from a tabloid.

It was of me standing on my tiptoes, kissing James on the nose. The tree was on the roof of our car. It was actually a really great photo. The only thing wrong with it was the caption under the picture: "Professor James Hunter and student caught fraternizing once again." I nuzzled into James' side. I was just going to pretend that the headline Rob made up was what it had really said. I never thought I'd get used to the tabloids. But maybe I finally was. Although, it was so unnerving that I hadn't even seen the paparazzi.

"Do you get alerts about us or something?" James asked.

"Of course," Rob said. "How do you expect me to keep up to date with you two when I live in boring old Delaware where nothing happens?"

"You could move back."

"Yeah. I guess I could."

I smiled to myself as I listened to their exchange. One day, I knew Rob would move back to New York. When he was ready to have some roots. But I couldn't imagine it being any time soon. Until then, I enjoyed his unexpected visits.

I took a sip of my hot chocolate and rested my head on James' shoulder. We didn't need a Christmas tree or any fancy decorations. I was perfectly content just being next to him.

Chapter 2

2 DAYS BEFORE CHRISTMAS

I pushed my cart through the aisle of the hardware store. Decorations of all kinds lined the aisle. I had already been here once, right after Thanksgiving. I had picked up tons of ornaments and lights. Tonight, we'd finally be putting them to use.

I stopped my cart by the Christmas tree stands. How I had forgotten one of these? Honestly, I knew the answer. Growing up, I never had to think about it. We just had one. But I was an adult now. I needed to start thinking two steps ahead. I lifted up one of the stands and examined it. I wasn't exactly sure what I was looking for. It seemed good enough.

"You ready to go?" Rob asked as he dumped some stuff into the cart.

I jumped. I'd been so lost in my own thoughts that I had completely forgotten he was roaming around the store too. "Um, do you think this one is good?" I held it out to him.

He picked it up and turned it around, twisting some of the little knobs sticking out. "How the hell should I know?" He tossed it into the cart.

I laughed. "What did you get?" I was about to reach into the cart when he slapped my hand.

"It's a surprise. No peeking."

Whatever it was, he had already bought it. It was in a plastic bag tied tight. "Is that my Christmas present?" I asked.

"Yeah. I figured I had to get you something good since you'll be giving me head come Christmas morning."

I'm pretty sure my face was scarlet. "What are you talking about? I never said that."

"Are you seriously not taking my advice? Every guy just wants head."

"Okay, maybe. But that just means maybe I'll give it to my fiancé. Not you."

"Perfect. I just tricked you into getting him the perfect gift." He thrust his hips forward suggestively. In the middle of the hardware store.

"Stop it," I said through my laughter. I hit his arm but he didn't stop thrusting. "You're completely ridiculous." I kept my head down to hide my embarrassment as I pushed my cart toward the checkout. But it didn't stop me from being aware of the flashing lights. God, the paparazzi were relentless. Usually they didn't follow me. They preferred to bother James to no end. After all, he was the famous one. Why did it seem like they weren't letting up recently?

Rob sensed my annoyance and stepped in front of me, blocking them from view as I checked out. I handed the cashier cash and tapped my foot nervously as I waited for the change.

"You're the girl," the cashier said. He snapped his fingers like he was trying to place me. "The one who slept with James Hunter."

What did he want me to say? Congratulations, you are correct? "I think you have the wrong person," I said instead as I grabbed the change he handed me.

He looked at the paparazzi and then back at me. "If you say so."

I loved James. I'd move to the ends of the earth for him. But sometimes I just hated New York. I grabbed my bag and walked as quickly as possible toward the car parked outside. Ian stepped out and opened up the door for me.

"Thank you," I said and ducked into the back seat. I exhaled the breath I had been holding as soon as Ian closed the door. James was right. It was really nice having Ian around.

Rob opened up the door on the other side and slid in next to me. "Where to next?"

"Home."

"Lame. Let's go do something fun."

"I have a million things to do before James gets home."

"Let's go get drunk and ice skate."

I laughed and stared at him. "Maybe you can call some of your friends to do that."

"Ugh. They're all working. We could meet up with some of your friends though. That's a great idea. Make sure to invite a single girl you want to set me up with."

I swallowed hard. "Oh. I mean...I feel like it's last minute. They're probably all busy."

He lowered his eyebrows slightly. I hated when he did that. It reminded me so much of James. And it made me just want to confess everything to him.

"You're such a liar," he said. "Have you seriously made no friends here?"

"No! I've made friends. There's Mason and Matt," I said, naming two of James' friends that hung out with us sometimes. "And you."

Rob's eyes seemed to grow. "Those aren't your friends, Penny. They're James'."

"And by association, they're mine too." I tried not to say it defensively, but it came out a little angry. "James and I hang out together in our free time. And everyone..." my voice trailed off. "Rumors spread, Rob. Just because we moved doesn't mean people stopped talking."

He gave me a sympathetic smile. "Home it is."

I looked down at my hands that were twisted in knots. "You can still go out and have fun tonight, though."

"Are you trying to get rid of me?"

"No."

"Your voice just got all weird and high pitched."

"No it didn't."

"You just did it again. I get the hint. You want some alone time with my little bro."

"Little bro? He's your older brother."

"But I'm bigger where it counts." He winked at me. His phone buzzed and he pulled it out of his pocket. He laughed. "Look. I'm famous." He showed me a picture of him thrusting in the middle of the hardware store, with my arm wrapped around his bicep.

"You were already famous." I grabbed his phone from him. "Torrid affair up in flames?" I said, quoting the article. "Seriously? Now they think I'm cheating on James with you?" I tossed the phone back at him.

He leaned forward slightly. "Well if they already think so..."

"Don't make me lace your hot chocolate."

He chuckled and leaned back in his seat. "I'll get out of your hair tonight. But seriously, Penny, talk to some of your classmates. I'm sure they're not all that bad."

I thought about how the whispers always seemed to stop when I entered a room. The way guys stared at me like I was easy. I didn't want to get to know them. And I didn't need to get to know them. I was perfectly happy just the way things were.

***

When I heard the key in the lock, I rewound the song to the beginning and ran over to the front door. "Merry Christmas Eve Eve!" I said as soon as James stepped into the apartment. I threw my arms around the back of his neck and attacked his face with kisses.

He laughed and planted his lips against mine. "What is all this?" he asked as he pulled away.

Believe by Josh Groban was blaring through the speakers, freshly baked cookies were sitting on the counter, and I had even somehow managed to get the tree into the stand without any help. Most importantly, I had also gotten Rob to spend the night out with friends. It was the romantic night I had wanted yesterday. "It's tree decorating night," I said. "Want a cookie?"

"You've been busy." He pulled off his scarf and gloves and gave me that smile that made my knees weak. "I'd love one. What kind?"

"Chocolate chip."

"With walnuts?"

"Of course. It's dessert after all." That was one of our things. We both thought desserts were better when they had nuts. I grabbed the plate from the kitchen and lifted it up to him.

He took a huge bite. "Delicious."

I smiled up at him. "If I'm being honest, Ellen gave me the recipe. But I made them by myself."

He grabbed another one off the plate. "They're amazing. Did Rob help you make them before or after you two fondled each other in aisle twelve?"

I choked on the bite I had just taken. "Neither." I quickly shook my head. "I mean, he didn't help me. And I didn't fondle him at the hardware store."

James smiled. "I know. I'm just kidding." He kissed my forehead. "But that picture circulating is rather incriminating."

"Are you getting those alerts now too? Please turn them off. I don't need a reminder every time something embarrassing happens to me." And I definitely didn't need to see what stupid caption they came up with next.

He lifted the plate of cookies out of my hand and placed it down on the kitchen counter. "Spill it."

"Spill what? You know, speaking of spills, do you want some milk? I'll try not to spill it though."

He laughed and pulled me against his chest before I could reach the fridge. "Talk to me."

"Why can't everyone just leave us alone, James? It's almost Christmas for goodness sakes. I mean, the cashier at the store didn't even wish me a Merry Christmas. He just asked if I was the girl that slept with James Hunter. What is it with people in New York?" I sighed as soon as I saw the expression on his face.

"Penny, if you're not happy here..."

I put my finger against his lips, silencing him. "I didn't mean it. I am happy. Can we just rewind to when you came in? I'll go start the song again." I tried to squirm out of his grip but he just held me tighter.

"Let's go to your parents' for Christmas," James said. "I think maybe spending a few days in Delaware might be just what we need."

I didn't need to go back to Delaware. I just needed him. "I want to start traditions together. I told you I wanted to spend Christmas with you in New York. And I meant it."

He stared down at me with his piercing brown eyes. I could tell he was analyzing my reaction. I just wasn't sure what he was searching for.

"I know you want me to tell you what I liked best about Christmas growing up. And how we can mold our traditions together. But I don't really know what to say. We didn't decorate the tree..."

"Trim the tree," I corrected him.

"Trim? Why would you want to cut the tree?"

"It's a phrase. You know...trimming the Christmas tree."

He stared at me with a blank expression on his face. "Yeah, you just made that up. Trimming a tree is cutting it."

"No, trimming a tree is decorating it. Look it up. It's a thing."

He smiled. "Okay. I'll take your word for it. We didn't *trim* the tree. We didn't hang stockings. We didn't necessarily do anything out of the ordinary. All I can really think of is that my dad used to read us *The Night Before Christmas.* I remember sitting around the tree with Rob and Jen and trying to pay attention but being so excited about Santa coming. But that's when I was really young. It's been a long time since I believed in the magic of Christmas."

"Then let's have Rob and Jen over for Christmas. It'll be just like when you were kids again." Rob was always over anyway. I had met Jen once and I really liked her. I'd be happy to share our Christmas with them.

"They can't come."

"But you didn't even ask them. I'm sure Rob will at least say yes."

James touched the side of my face. He suddenly looked sad. "They're going to my parents'."

"I thought you said they weren't doing a Christmas gathering this year?"

He didn't have to say it. I could see it all over his face.

"They're still having it," I said. "*I'm* just not invited." It stung. His parents' rejection always stung.

"No. No," he said a little more firmly. "*We're* not invited."

"They uninvited you because of me."

He laughed. "They uninvited me because I yelled at them about being assholes. It has nothing to do with you. You, Penny, are perfect. And if they don't want to meet you, it's their loss. Not the other way around. Trust me."

I had been living in the city for a couple months now. His parents refused to meet me. It was like I was so below them that I wasn't worth their very valuable time. "Do you want to go? I mean, if you want to go for a little while, I can just..."

"Penny, I would never leave you alone on Christmas."

For some reason my mind focused on the words "alone on Christmas." We had talked about his parents sucking plenty of times. And I didn't want them to ruin our Christmas Eve Eve. "Home Alone or The Grinch?" I asked and took a step back from him. "And I mean The Grinch with Jim Carrey, not the cartoon version. Oh, or Elf!"

He raised his eyebrow. "For?"

"What do you mean for? To watch while we trim the tree. And to get so distracted that we really just end up on the couch eating all those cookies I just baked." I grabbed the plate of cookies and then with my free hand pulled him into the living room. "And before you respond, think about it. There is a correct answer."

"I've seen Home Alone. But I've never seen the other two. You seemed excited about Elf. We could watch that. Who's in it?"

I set the cookies down on the coffee table. "I feel like I don't even know you right now. Elf is the greatest movie of all time. Will Ferrell is in it. Who hasn't seen Elf? It's a classic!"

He laughed. "I'm not that much older than you, but I'm pretty sure that doesn't count as a classic. It's still fairly new."

I turned off the Christmas music and grabbed the remote. "You're insane. And FYI, the correct answer was that we should watch all of them."

"All of them? How long does it take to decorate the tree?"

"It takes a long time to *trim* the tree because you're supposed to get distracted and watch the movies the whole time." I switched on Elf. "Time for a lesson in all things Christmassy, Professor Hunter."

He laughed and pulled me onto his lap.

***

"A little to the left," James said.

I leaned slightly to the side and hung the ornament on a branch. "You're an expert now?" The credits from Elf were rolling and I had just turned on the Christmas music again. James had been so engrossed in the movie, that we hadn't hung up a single ornament.

"I'm an expert on the angle your butt looks best in."

I laughed and turned around. "Help me instead of just watching me." I grabbed his hand, but instead of pulling him up he pulled me back onto the couch.

"I like watching you," he whispered against my ear and then lightly bit my earlobe.

I swallowed down the moan threatening to escape my throat. I had barely put up half the ornaments. And we had only watched one of the movies. We still had so much to do to make our apartment look festive.

He bit my earlobe again as his fingers trailed along the hem of my sweater, dipping dangerously close to my ass.

"I didn't realize how much Elf could turn someone on," I said.

He laughed. His hot breath tickled my neck.

God, he was so distracting.

"I don't think I've ever seen you happier than at this very moment," he whispered. His hands wandered up beneath the back of my sweater.

"I love Christmas. And I love you. What's there to not be happy about?"

He kissed me slow. I had the realization that this was the first time I had ever been with someone during Christmas. The first time anyone had kissed me while listening to my favorite Christmas songs. The first time I had ever been in love during the most magical time of year.

He shifted, pushing me down on the couch and positioning himself between my thighs. His kisses were more passionate now as his hands slid to my breasts. And I had the sensation that he was showing me just how much he loved me. I didn't try to repress my moan this time.

I forgot about the box of ornaments. And the cocoa going cold. Because the only thing I loved more than Christmas was James. I was engaged to this beautiful man. If this was how he wanted to enjoy the Christmas festivities, I could give him this. I could give him this over and over again until he loved Christmas as much as I did.

Chapter 3

CHRISTMAS EVE

So far, our Christmas traditions included being third-wheeled by Rob and drinking too much hot cocoa. And then making love underneath a half decorated Christmas tree. I could get behind these new traditions. But that didn't mean the tree had to go untrimmed.

I placed the last ornament onto a branch and stepped back. The weight of the ornaments had caused the tree to appear even more lopsided. I smiled. It was perfect.

I looked at the gifts I had wrapped earlier that were now sitting under the tree. I sighed. None of them were right. My eyes landed on the chess set. It was a stupid gift because I knew he'd beat me every time we played until I got sick of losing and stopped wanting to play. I had also bought a cook book and a knife set because I wanted to start cooking together. Although I knew the first thing out of his mouth was going to be that we had Ellen for that. My retaliation was going to be that we didn't have her to cook for us on the weekends. But that would probably just insult him because he'd always make me Eggo waffles in the morning. Which I loved. God, why was I so bad at giving gifts?

I need James to believe in the magic of Christmas again. These gifts aren't going to cut it. I giggled to myself because I had gotten him knives. *Stop it.* I needed to focus. I grabbed my laptop and sat down on the couch. In just a moment I had the listing up on Amazon for *The Night Before Christmas.* But it was Christmas Eve. I couldn't get a copy shipped this late.

Which meant I'd need to venture out into the cold. Into the paparazzi territory. I turned off my laptop. Maybe I could get Rob to go with me. He was never annoyed by the limelight.

I walked over to the guest bedroom and knocked on the door. There was no answer. It was almost noon. How much longer could Rob sleep? I knocked again. "Rob?"

No answer.

Please don't be naked. I opened up the door and peered in. I had only woken up an hour after James left. And Rob had never been an early riser. Had he not come home last night? I walked back out into the living room and grabbed my purse. I felt like such a mom, but I clicked on his name in my phone and put it up to my ear.

He answered after a few rings. "Hey, sexy, what's up?"

Normally I'd berate him for calling me that, but I was just happy that he was alive. "Where are you? I went to your room and you weren't there. You almost made me freak out."

He laughed. "I know I'm always on your mind, but don't worry, I'm fine. Just out."

"Okay." That was a vague answer. "I need your help. I was thinking about getting James..."

"Head."

Ugh. "No." *Well, maybe.* "I want to get him a copy of *The Night Before Christmas* like your dad read to you when you were little. Do you remember what edition it was? Or who illustrated it?"

"Um. I don't know. That was forever ago."

That was helpful. "You can't remember anything about it?"

"I didn't say that. It was a pop-up book. And it was blue."

I could work with that. "Okay, thanks, Rob. I was going to go out and look for a copy, do you want to come?"

"Can't sweets, I'm busy. But I'll see you tonight for anti-Christmas."

"What's anti-Christmas?"

But there was no response. He had already hung up. *Weird.* I wasn't surprised though. Most of my conversations with Rob were strange.

I pulled a knit hat low on my head and tucked my red hair beneath my coat as I pulled it on. The best part about the freezing cold winter was that I could at least go a little incognito. Hopefully the paparazzi would leave me alone.

***

After going to two Barnes and Nobles and finally talking to someone helpful, I found out that whatever edition I was looking for was probably out of print. Which I probably should have realized. If James' father read it to him as a kid, it was probably published before I was even born.

I stepped into the used bookstore and smiled at the little bell that jingled above my head. The whole store was decorated for Christmas. I breathed in slowly. There was nothing better than the smell of books. Especially ones that had already been loved. And mixed with the smell of cinnamon in the air, I felt like I was in a Christmas dream of mine.

"Merry Christmas!" said a cheery older woman with long gray hair almost to her waist. She bustled over to me. "Would you like a cup of tea or coffee while you browse?"

"I would love a cup of tea." I pulled off my hat. The little store's heat was blasting.

Her eyes grew big for a moment, but the look of surprise quickly vanished. "Very well. I'll be right back." She hurried off in the direction she had come.

I smiled. She had clearly recognized me. But she didn't ask me questions. Or make me feel belittled. I was pretty sure this was my new favorite store. I looked at the shelves covered with books along the wall first. There seemed to be no rhyme or reason to the way they were organized. It looked like they were alphabetical by author's last name but then it would switch to being alphabetical by book title.

"Here you are," the woman said and handed me a mug.

"Thank you so much."

"Is there anything I can help you find?" she asked.

"Yes, actually. I'm looking for an edition of *The Night Before Christmas* from the late 80's. Well, I think it's probably from the late 80's. I'm not really sure. It's a blue pop-up book, but I can't remember the illustrator."

She snapped her fingers. "I think you're in luck."

I followed her through one of the aisles to a cart in the back of the store.

"This just came in today," she said and lifted a large hardback book off the cart.

There was a ribbon in the center of it, tying the two sides together. It was blue. I set my tea down and lifted the book out of her hands.

"It's illustrated by Tom Patrick. It was a Hallmark edition that came out in 1988."

I untied the ribbon and opened up the book. The first page had a bed pop-up with children sleeping. You could even turn the sugarplum pictures above their head. It was the most adorable interactive pop-up book I had ever seen. Really, it put every other children's book to shame. It was so intricate.

"Do you think that's the one?" the woman asked.

"I think it must be." A few pages looked worn, like it had been loved before. But it was still in great condition. James was going to love it. "I'll take it," I said.

The woman smiled. "Anything else I can help you find?"

"No, this was exactly what I needed. I can't believe this just came in today."

"The magic of Christmas," she said with a smile. "Do you want it gift wrapped?"

"That would be fantastic." I handed her the book and followed her to the front of the store as I sipped my tea. Even the tea was amazing. It was probably where the smell of cinnamon swirling around the shop was coming from.

"I'm pretty sure this is my new favorite store," I said as I watched her elegantly wrap the book with a bow and everything.

"I'm glad to hear it." She cut the ends of the bow and got change for the cash I handed her. She gave me the bag and then my change. "Merry Christmas, dear."

I smiled. "Merry Christmas. And thank you for this. I was searching everywhere for it. This is going to mean the world to my fiancé."

"I think your story is beautiful," the woman said right before I pushed through the exit. I stopped and turned back toward her.

"I'm sorry, I don't mean to speak out of place. I just...I see the tabloids. And I know it's probably hard. But don't let the people who don't understand the first thing about love get you down." She gave me a kind smile. "Be grateful every day that God pushed you two together. Especially during the holidays. What a joyous time to be thankful."

"Thank you," I said. She had made my eyes tear up. How did she know I was struggling?

How did she know how badly I needed to hear that? I had the eeriest feeling that if I came back in a week the store would be gone. That I had just imagined it into existence. The most perfect little store. With the kindest old woman. It almost felt like she was me from the future. Giving myself advice.

"Merry Christmas, dear."

"Merry Christmas." I gave her one last smile and the bell jingled above my head as I walked back outside. Not everyone in New York was so bad. Maybe I was the Grinch. And maybe my heart had just grown two sizes today.

***

I pulled the change the bookstore owner had given me out of my purse when I saw a Salvation Army Santa set up on the sidewalk outside the store. He hadn't been there when I walked in. He was ringing his bell and had such a big smile on his face. He wasn't like the other Santa impersonators I had seen collecting money for the past few weeks. He looked real. His beard didn't even seem fake. He had the rosy cheeks and everything. Although, my cheeks were probably rosy too from the cold.

I stepped up to him and placed the change into his basket. Maybe the spirit of Christmas the shop owner had given me would spread to him next.

"Merry Christmas," Santa said and continued to ring his bell.

"Merry Christmas, Santa." It sounded silly saying it aloud. Santa wasn't real. He was a part of my childhood that I still held on to in my heart though. And I had never seen a more realistic impersonator.

He rung his bell again and winked at me, like he could read my thoughts.

I smiled and continued to walk down the sidewalk. It was fitting that he had suddenly appeared outside the store that held the most Christmas spirit. I turned around to see him once more, but he was blocked from view from all the people on the sidewalk. It was almost like he had disappeared.

I pulled my hat down a little lower and kept walking. It took every ounce of restraint to stop myself from humming Christmas carols. This was going to be the best Christmas Eve ever. I could just feel it.

My feet stopped in front of a department store window. There were stockings hung along a fake fireplace. I suddenly had the best idea. I pushed through the doors. There were still a few hours before James would come home. That gave me plenty of time to figure out a way to make him believe Santa was still real.

First came the stockings. Then some of his favorite dark chocolate candy. *What else did Santa always put in my stocking?* I smiled to myself. I should have asked myself what my parents had put in my stocking. But today I was a believer. I grabbed a few other things and walked over to the closest checkout.

Which just so happened to be by the lingerie section. My feet stopped on their own accord again. *Head.* Was Rob right? Was that all that James really wanted? I thought about last night. And how he had ended up on top of me instead of putting a star on the top of our tree. I bit my lip. It wouldn't hurt to look to see if they had anything good.

I wandered through the section until I came to a sexy corset thing with garters in what could only be described as a sexy Mrs. Claus costume. I paused, but only for a second. If I was being Santa, I needed the outfit to go with it. I grabbed my size. I didn't have time to try it on. James would be home soon and I needed to wrap the new presents and get ready for dinner. We were going out to some fancy restaurant he said had the best Christmas Eve dinner. I wasn't sure what that meant. Christmas Eve dinner wasn't a big thing at my house. I'm pretty sure I just ate cookies the night before Christmas.

But I wasn't going to be late. It was the one thing so far he had told me he wanted to do. Everything else was just me trying to force him to do things I did growing up. I draped the Mrs. Claus costume on top of the other things in my basket.

Well, one thing was for sure. I definitely didn't wear anything like this on previous Christmases. New Christmas tradition - check.

***

I reached behind my back to try to zipper my dress up the rest of the way. Usually I had James do it for me. But this dress was so low cut in the back that I was able to zipper it myself. I stared at my reflection in the mirror. The dress was low cut in the front too. I had found the perfect red lipstick to match the red shade of my dress. And I'm pretty sure I was wearing more mascara and eyeliner than I ever had in my life. Melissa had been sending me YouTube makeup tutorials. I had taken the hint and tried to learn a few things. I took a deep breath. James was going to love this.

I started to hum *It's Beginning to Look a Lot Like Christmas* as I pulled on my stilettos. Tonight was going to be the best Christmas Eve either one of us could possibly have. I just knew it. I heard the front door open and I rushed to the stairs.

"Merry Christmas Eve, James!" I yelled from the top.

He appeared at the bottom of the stairs with a huge smile and an arrangement of poinsettias in red and white.

I made my way down as quickly as my heels allowed.

"I'm pretty sure all my Christmas dreams have already come true," he said. "You're breathtakingly beautiful." He grabbed my hand and spun me in a circle.

I smiled up to him as he pulled me against his chest.

"Merry Christmas Eve, baby." He ran the tip of his nose down the length of mine.

"I'm so excited I can barely stand it," I said. "And you even bought a Christmas decoration." I lifted the flowers out of his hand. "They're beautiful."

He didn't say anything. I turned around to see him staring at my legs.

"Is it too short? You didn't mention the name of the restaurant so I couldn't look it up. If it's not appropriate..."

"Penny, you look absolutely stunning. I was staring because I can't take my eyes off you."

"You look very handsome yourself." And he did. He was wearing a dark suit with a green tie. I loved the tiny bit of Christmas spirit in his outfit.

His phone started ringing, but he ignored it. "Ready to go?" he asked.

"Aren't you going to answer your phone?"

"No, I already know it's Rob." He grabbed my hand and pulled me toward the door.

"And you're not answering it because...?"

"Because I already have plans with you."

"Oh, James, does he usually come with you to your Christmas Eve dinner? He can come if you want. I want tonight to be exactly what you want."

"And I want to spend the evening with you. Besides, this place is supposed to have amazing food."

I stopped in the foyer. "Haven't you eaten there before? I thought this was a thing you used to do every Christmas Eve."

He laughed. "No. The restaurant only opened a few years ago. I just thought you'd like it."

I didn't even know what to say. So I just blinked at him. How had I completely misread his idea for tonight? "What do you usually do on Christmas Eve?"

"The guys do this anti-Christmas thing. It's not important."

He did have a tradition. We were finally getting somewhere. "Rob mentioned that earlier. What is anti-Christmas?"

"It's just what it sounds like. It's the anti-Christmas. It's hanging out with your friends instead of family. Drinking too much to prepare for the horrors of the next day."

The horrors? Of Christmas? Was he insane? Was I engaged to a complete lunatic? I blinked again. "You do hate Christmas," I said.

"I don't hate Christmas."

"Then why have an anti-Christmas on Christmas Eve?"

James shrugged. "You know Mason's relationship with his parents is strained." He didn't offer anything else.

"And yours with your parents," I said softly.

"Yeah."

His favorite memory of Christmas was his father reading to him. And now he hated Christmas because his relationship with his parents wasn't good. I couldn't fix that relationship. They wouldn't even meet me. But I could take his mind off of it. Anti-Christmas seemed like the best way to do that. Besides, he had finally shared a tradition with me. I wanted to experience it with him. "Let's do anti-Christmas."

He laughed. "Penny, we have reservations. Let's get going so that we're not late."

"Screw the reservations. I want in on this tradition."

"Penny, nothing about you is anti-Christmas."

"So teach me," I said.

"As much as I love teaching you lessons, I don't want to teach you not to have Christmas spirit."

"Well good, because you probably can't. But if doing this anti-Christmas thing is what you usually do, I want to do it. To new traditions, right?"

He raised his left eyebrow. "Are you sure?"

"Absolutely."

***

It turns out, I absolutely wasn't sure. The bar was dimly lit. And they weren't even playing

Christmas music. What kind of place didn't play Christmas music on Christmas Eve?

The guy at the door stamped my hand to show that I was underage. Not that I wanted to drink. I wanted to wake up on Christmas morning refreshed and ready to go super early. I was itching to run back out into the chilly winter air. And insist on going ice skating by the Rockefeller tree. Or listen to the carolers we had passed by on the way here. Or drag him to church so we could sing the songs I looked forward to every year.

But I didn't say any of that. For the next hour or so...*will it be that long?*...I was going to do anti-Christmas. Bah, humbug!

We wound our way through the other patrons until we found his friends at table in the back.

"You came!" Rob shouted. "I told you they'd come. Pay up." He put his hand out.

"What the hell are you doing here?" Mason groaned. "You said you were going out to dinner." He slapped a stack of way too many bills into Rob's hand.

"Yeah, we all thought you were totally whipped," Matt added. He forked over a wad of cash to Rob.

"Do you guys make bets on our relationship?" I asked.

"Usually only how long it'll last," Mason said with a laugh.

I knew he was joking. *Right?* I liked James' friends. But Mason still kinda gave me the creeps. He always had a look in his eyes like he was judging me. Or my body. Or something. I couldn't quite put my finger on it. But just like with Rob, I was getting used to him. And Matt was always nice to me.

I sat down in the stool that James pulled out for me and let him take my coat.

"Ow, ow!" Rob yelled. "You really dressed up for us."

"For him," I said and pointed over my shoulder where James was hanging up our jackets.

"Sure," Rob whispered and leaned forward slightly. "I told the guys we're all getting lucky tonight because you're handing out blowjobs for Christmas."

What. The. Actual. Fuck. Why was he hell-bent on embarrassing me all the time? "Rob, for the millionth time, I am not putting my mouth anywhere near your penis."

"Well, that's good to hear," James said with a laugh as he sat down next to me. "Do you guys want another round?"

"Absolutely," Mason said. "Let me help you grab it. What'll you have, Penny?"

"Ginger Ale if they have it." My stomach suddenly felt upset. I needed carols. And snow. And to watch The Grinch, not be sitting with four of them.

When they came back with the drinks I took a sip and set it down. "Okay. So now what? Do we all talk about how much we hate Christmas?"

"No." Matt threw his hands over his ears. "We don't mention that word at all."

"Rob just said it a few minutes ago when he mentioned blowjobs."

"Blowjobs?" Rob said with a smile. "Who said anything about blowjobs? Are you suggesting something, Penny?"

I rolled my eyes. "So we just sit here and don't talk about tomorrow at all? So it's just like a normal day?"

"Exactly," Mason said. "A normal day where it's totally fine to be fighting with your parents and not be in a relationship."

"Okay, someone's had too much to drink," Matt said and pulled away Mason's whiskey glass. "Did you seriously just imply that you wish you were dating someone?"

Mason looked at me and James and then grabbed his glass back. "No."

Yes, maybe it was unnerving that it always seemed like Mason was assessing me. But he was sad that he was going to be alone on Christmas. And that broke my heart. He was lonely. Is that why they were all here? Because they were single on Christmas Eve?

"I have an idea," I said. "And please forgive me in advance because I'm about to say Christmas a bunch of times."

Matt groaned.

I looked over at James and he was smiling at me.

I turned back to the group. "I think you guys should let me hijack anti-Christmas. And show you what Christmas Eve is supposed to be like. Because this," I said and gestured to the sad bar, "is not what Christmas is all about. The only thing you've got right is that we're all together. So let's stop getting drunk and go have fun out there."

No one said anything.

"It's Christmas Eve, guys. It only comes around once a year. We can do this the day after Christmas. Please. I promise it'll be fun." I glanced back at James.

"I'll get our coats," he said. "You guys in?"

"Fine," Mason said. "But I'm not singing."

Matt pushed back his stool. "Ditto."

Rob downed the rest of his drink. "Let's Christmas Eve the shit out of everything."

"That's the spirit," I said. *I guess.*

***

They weren't fans of listening to carolers. But I had kind of expected that. If it had been snowing it would have been easy to entertain them with a snow ball fight. The Christmas angels were holding back on me, though.

"There!" I said and pointed at a cute little stand selling roasted chestnuts. "I've always wanted to try those. Have you ever?"

James shook his head.

"You've lived in the city growing up and never once had a roasted chestnut? Are you insane? If they had them in Wilmington I would have tried them." I stopped by the stand and ordered some for all of us.

I popped one in my mouth. It was surprisingly sweet. Not at all nutty tasting like I was expecting.

"It kinda tastes like a sweet potato," Rob said and then spit it out on the ground.

I laughed. "Not a fan of sweet potatoes?"

"Not at all."

"It's actually pretty good," James said.

Mason elbowed him in the side. "You would like nuts in your mouth." But then he ate his. "Eh, it's alright."

"Not bad," Matt said. "What's next?" He stared at me expectantly. He seemed to be enjoying this the most. I had a suspicion that he wasn't a huge fan of anti-Christmas.

"Do you guys want to go ice skating?" I asked.

"Ugh, why are you torturing us?" Rob groaned.

"Rob, you asked if I wanted to go earlier today."

"That was when I thought you'd be bringing some of your hot single friends."

Right. Before he found out that I hadn't made any friends. Except for these guys. And damn it, I was going to force them to have fun tonight if it was the last thing I did. "Ice skating. Now." I said it with way too much authority. It made it sound like what I was forcing them to do wouldn't be any fun at all. I pointed to the Rockefeller tree when no one moved.

They all groaned and pretending like I was torturing them. Was I? This wasn't the night they had planned.

"Are they going to hate me after this?" I asked James as we followed them toward the ice.

"Are you kidding?"

I looked up at him. "No? It seems like I'm torturing them."

"What? They're having a blast."

"They're literally groaning."

He laughed. "They're just messing with you, Penny. If they weren't having fun they would have gone back to the bar. When we left, Rob even said, 'if this blows, let's just head back to the bar.' But they're all still here."

I smiled. "Are you having fun?"

"I'm having the best Christmas Eve ever. Now let's get you in a pair of skates so I can watch that perfect ass of yours continuously fall on the ice."

"I'm a good ice skater," I said.

"Well I'm not."

I laughed as he wrapped his arm behind my back. I snuggled into his warmth as we followed our friends.

Mason was standing there watching Rob and Matt lace their skates.

"Aren't you going to join us?" I asked.

"Actually, I should get going. I have a couple errands to run."

"You sure, man?" Matt said. "It's going to be just like old times. We used to do this with my mom when we were little," he said to me.

Maybe I was the only one that saw it, but Mason looked sad. I knew he was fighting with his parents. I knew this Christmas was hard for him.

"I'll catch you all later," Mason said and started to walk away.

No Merry Christmas. No cheer at all. He just walked away. But he didn't get far before I caught up to him.

"Mason!"

He turned around.

"I'm sorry, I didn't know you used to do this with your parents."

He parted his lips like he was about to say something, but then he closed them again. He didn't have to say anything. I knew he was hurting.

"Come to our house tomorrow for Christmas," I said. "James and I would love to have you."

"I don't want to impose..."

"You wouldn't be imposing. I know you like to look like you're made of steel, but I know you're all warm and fuzzy on the inside. And guess what? Earlier today, Rob made fun of me because I haven't made any friends in New York. But do you know what I told him? That I made friends with you."

He smiled. "But Christmas is for family."

"I left my family behind in Wilmington." It hurt to say out loud, but it was true. "But do you know what I've been learning? Friends are family that you choose. Come tomorrow. We can miss our parents together."

It was almost like he thawed in front of me. "Yeah, I mean...if you're sure."

"I'm sure." I wrapped him in a huge hug. "Merry Christmas Eve, Mason."

"Merry Christmas Eve, Penny."

This time when he walked away, he didn't look so sad. He even turned around and waved.

"What was all that about?" James asked when I ran back over to him. He already had his skates laced and was holding a pair out for me.

"I invited him over tomorrow. I hope that's okay." I sat down and started lacing my skates.

"Of course it's okay."

"I like your friends, James."

"I'm pretty sure they like you too."

I looked out at the ice and laughed as Matt pushed Rob. Rob fell right on his ass.

"Shall we?" James said and put out his hand.

I slid my hand into his and let him guide me over to the skating rink. New York was truly starting to feel like home. I even had this new amazing family. I smiled again at Matt and Rob fighting on the ice.

Whatever I remembered about ice skating was completely wrong. Because I landed on my ass almost as many times as James. Partially because I kept insisting on holding his hand, though. So whenever he fell, he took me with him.

"Race you!" Rob yelled.

I picked up my pace and quickly realized I didn't know how to stop. I did the best I could to slow down before colliding straight into James.

He laughed as we tumbled onto the ice.

"Ow. I think you're trying to break my back," he groaned.

I smiled and placed a soft kiss against his lips. "No, I like you in one piece, thank you very much."

A smile spread across his face. Pure Christmas joy.

"What?" I asked. I wanted to know what caused that smile. Because I wanted to see it over and over again.

"Penny, it's snowing."

Just as he said the words, I saw a snowflake land on his forehead. I looked up at the sky. Flurries were falling slowly. It felt like a Christmas miracle. *Snow! It's really snowing!*

"If it wasn't freezing, I could stay in this moment forever," James said.

I smiled down at him. "And why's that?"

"You. That smile on your face."

I swallowed hard. "I guess we need to get you some hot chocolate to warm you up." I lifted my finger and tapped the tip of his nose. "Boop." As soon as I did it, I was completely mortified. *God, did I just do that? I just booped James Hunter on the nose. Who boops James Hunter on the nose?*

"Did you just boop me on the nose?" he said with a laugh.

"Um, no. I think you imagined that."

He tickled my side as I tried to climb off of him and I slipped on the ice, landing beside him. "Fine. I booped your nose. I confess." I couldn't help but laugh.

"That was the cutest thing ever."

I didn't even mind him describing me as cute tonight. It was Christmas Eve. And Christmas Eve was always perfect. Besides, I didn't just boop James Hunter's nose. I booped my fiancé's nose. It was good that we were learning all the weird things we did.

***

"So...did I succeed?" I asked as we all blew on our hot chocolate.

"I'm a believer in Christmas miracles," Rob said sarcastically. "I'm officially done with anti-Christmas." That sounded more serious. "But really, we should still all get together on Christmas Eve. But we should do this stuff instead."

Matt smiled. "I'd be down for that. This is a much better tradition."'

James pulled me into his side. "Count me in too. Christmas Eve only comes around once a year. We might as well celebrate it in style."

I felt like my smile couldn't get any bigger.

"And you guys should come over tomorrow whenever you can," James said. "Mason's already coming."

One big happy family. It felt like my heart definitely grew. There was no Grinch in me whatsoever. And as I looked around at all of them, I was pretty sure I didn't see one Grinch.

"We should probably get going though," James said. "It's getting pretty late. It'll be Christmas before we know it."

We said our goodbyes and walked hand in hand back toward our apartment. The snow was picking up, making our shoes leave a trail in the snow.

"This is magical, isn't it?" I said.

"It really is." He looked up. "I can't remember the last time it snowed on Christmas Eve or Christmas."

"I only remember it happening once. My family always went to midnight mass. And one time, we walked out afterwards, and snow started to fall. It felt like the clouds had been holding their breath and only released it once we were ready to see it. It was magical. Just like this."

"We could make a service. If you want to." He stopped me outside our apartment.

I shook my head. James wasn't religious. And I had stopped going to church every Sunday once I started college. "Actually, I want to give you something. If you'll open one of your presents early." I raised both my eyebrows, hoping he could tell how excited I was.

He got a boyish grin on his face. "I'm not going to complain about that."

The way he said it made it seem like he was expecting sex. I shouldn't have looked so overwhelmingly excited, but I couldn't help myself. I pulled him onto the elevator. I just hoped he reacted differently toward the book than Mason had reacted to ice skating. *Please don't be upset by this.*

We walked into our apartment and I turned on the Christmas music. I scanned through the songs until I found *Let it Snow*. I grabbed the book from under the tree and turned around.

He wasn't even looking at the present. He was just looking at me.

"Do you know how loved I feel when you look at me like that?" I asked as I stepped toward him.

"Like you're the most loved human being on this planet?" He tucked a loose strand of hair behind my ear. "Because you are."

His words were making me tear up. But I didn't want to cry. I never wanted to stop smiling. "I love you just as much." My words weren't eloquent, but I meant them. I thrust the present into his arms. "Open it." It was the first Christmas present I had ever given him. It felt momentous. I bit the inside of my lip as he tore the paper off.

A smile broke over his face. "This was the exact edition my dad used to read us." He untied the bow on the front of the book and opened it up. "How did you know?"

"Rob told me it was a pop-up book. And that it was blue. I found this really cute used bookstore and the woman that owned it said this book had just come in today."

He ran his finger along the little paper wheel that spun the sugarplums on the page. He laughed and looked up at me. "Penny, this is amazing. I can't believe you found it."

"Do you want me to read it to you?"

He laughed. "No, you've got to experience it for yourself. I'll read it to you." He grabbed my hand and pulled me over to the couch. He balanced the book on his knee and put his arm around my back.

As the snow fell outside and as the lights twinkled on our tree, he read to me. We only paused to play with the interactive pop-ups. And even though it was a story for parents to read to their kids, it didn't feel that way with us. Him reading it to me just made me feel loved. Like he wanted to share one of his happiest memories with me. It made me feel so close to him.

"Happy Christmas to all, and to all a good-night!" James said in a very deep voice.

I smiled up at him. "You really liked it?"

He kissed my temple. "I loved it. This was the most thoughtful gift anyone has ever given me."

I put my hand on his chest and felt the thudding of his heart beating. "We should probably get to bed so that Santa can come."

He laughed.

When I didn't say anything, he narrowed his eyes at me.

"Wait, are you serious? Penny we need to have a serious conversation. Santa isn't..."

I put my finger against his lips. "Don't say it, James. Don't say it until you wake up tomorrow and know for sure." I grabbed one of my notebooks off the coffee table and handed it to him. "Write down what you want from him and I'll get the milk and cookies."

"Baby, this is..."

"Awesome? Fantastic? The best thing ever?" I came back out carrying a plate of cookies and a glass of milk and set them down on the coffee table.

He laughed. "I was going to say ridiculous." But he ripped out the sheet of paper he had written on from the notebook and put it down next to the cookies and milk.

I grabbed the stockings I had stashed under the tree and hung mine up on the mantel of the fireplace. "Hang up your stocking too." I held it out to him.

He smiled as he got up off the couch. Our stockings had our names embroidered on them. I had been lucky that they had ones with our names left in the store on Christmas Eve. He shook his head as he hung up the stocking. "This really is ridiculous. But thank you for the stocking."

I grabbed the notebook, quickly wrote what I wanted, and placed the letter beside James'. "We'll see who's ridiculous come morning."

He lightly slapped my ass as he followed me up the stairs.

"Oh, actually, I'm thirsty," I said when I reached the top of the stairs. "I'm going to go grab some water. You can start getting ready for bed." I kissed his cheek and watched him go into our bedroom before I sprinted back down the stairs.

I pulled out the bag I had hidden under the Christmas tree. James was going to be so surprised when he woke up. I put the small presents I got for him inside of his stocking. I had bought a few random items for myself too, just to make it look like Santa didn't hate me. I tossed those into my stocking and then turned toward the coffee table. Even though I wasn't hungry, I quickly stuffed the cookies in my mouth and downed the milk.

I couldn't help but take a peek at James' note. I smiled when I saw that he had actually addressed it to Santa.

Dear Santa,

What is my Christmas wish? Well, that's an easy one. My wish to you is for Penny to truly feel like this is her home. For her to adjust to the city and be happy to be here with me. That is my Christmas wish.

-James

I held the sheet up to my chest. *I am happy.* And tomorrow I'd make sure he knew it. He wasn't the only one who had asked for something sentimental. I had asked Santa to give James the Christmas spirit. Because if there was anyone I knew that deserved the joy of Christmas in their heart, it was him.

I hurried back upstairs before James could suspect anything. As I crawled into bed after brushing my teeth, I snuggled into his side.

"Merry Christmas Eve, James," I whispered.

"Merry Christmas Eve, baby."

I closed my eyes. It had been years since I had been this excited for Christmas morning. When I finally drifted to sleep, the last thing I remembered was wondering if this was how my parents felt when they pretended to be Santa.

Chapter 4
CHRISTMAS

Just like every Christmas, my eyes flew open early. I turned toward the alarm clock. It was only 7 am. But I couldn't wait another second. I tried to hide my squeal of excitement as I slipped out from underneath James' arm and tiptoed to the bathroom.

I opened up the drawer in the bathroom vanity where I had stashed the naughty Mrs. Claus outfit. After I finally managed to clasp every little hook on the back of the corset, I turned around. I smiled. It was even better than my red dress from last night. Actually, it was way better. My boobs nearly reached my chin. James almost always woke up with morning wood. And this morning, I was going to use that to my advantage.

I zipped up my thigh high boots and finished the outfit with a Santa hat. This year I was the ho in ho, ho, ho. I walked out of the bathroom and over to James' side of the bed. "Merry Christmas, James."

He started to yawn but it sounded like more of a gasp by the time it was over. "Holy shit, Penny." He wiped the sleepy out of his eyes. "You have no idea how many times I wished I could wake up to this on Christmas morning growing up."

I laughed.

He blinked, like he thought he was imagining me.

"I heard you've been a little more naughty than nice this year."

"So I was sent you?" He pushed the covers back and sat up in bed.

I moved closer to him, putting my hands on his knees. "Mhm."

"Then I think I should be naughty more often."

"You could be naughty right now. Merry Christmas, James."

"This feels more like my birthday than Christmas." He slid off the bed and moved around me, effectively sandwiching me against the side of the bed. "How naughty are we talking?"

"As naughty as you want. When on the naughty list, I say live it up."

"You know, I probably do deserve to be on that list." He slowly trailed his fingers up the inside of my thigh. "Rumor has it I slept with one of my students."

"That's very naughty of you."

He pushed my thong to the side but didn't touch me. God, he had a way of making me go crazy with want.

"Oh you haven't heard the half of it," he said.

"Then tell me more." My head dropped back as he lightly brushed his finger against my wetness.

"I fell in love with her."

"More," I moaned.

"I asked her to marry me." He thrust a finger inside of me.

"James!"

He moved his hand faster. "Baby you have no idea what you do to me." Another finger joined the first, stretching me wide. "And do you know the naughtiest part?" he whispered in my ear.

My breath caught in my throat as I waited for his response.

"I still get hard when she calls me Professor Hunter."

I was seconds away from shattering.

"I need to taste you," he said and removed his fingers.

I wanted his mouth on me. There was no better feeling than his tongue. But this wasn't about me. This was a gift for him. And damn it, Rob was right. James clearly wanted head. And I wanted to give it to him.

"Naughty boys don't get what they want," I said and dropped to my knees. Before he had time to react I wrapped my fingers around the base of his cock and circled my tongue around his tip.

"Penny," he groaned.

I wrapped my lips around him and took him all the way to the back of my throat.

"Fuck." His fingers tangled into my hair, knocking my Santa hat to the ground.

He let me set the pace for a few more seconds before guiding me. I loved when he did that. When he used me for his pleasure. I loved how I could make him lose all control.

I tightened my lips.

He groaned again and quickly pulled my head back. "Hands on the bed and spread your thighs, gorgeous."

I followed his instructions. I was done with the role playing. He could have me however he wanted. He pressed down on the center of my back, making me lift my ass higher into the air.

"God, how did I get so lucky?" He pushed up the fabric of the short skirt and ran his hand over my bare ass, playing with the straps of the garter.

"James," I begged. Yes, this was his present. But I needed him inside of me. I couldn't wait any longer.

I felt my thong snap against my leg as he ripped it off. The feeling instantly made me even wetter. I waited for him to remove my garter belt, but instead he grabbed my hips and thrust into me. Hard.

A cry of satisfaction fell from my lips.

"You've been naughty too," he said.

"It's true. I fell in love with my professor." I bit my lip and tried to look as seductive as possible as I looked at him over my shoulder.

He thrust into me even harder.

I gripped the sheets, getting ready for the rest of the ride.

But then he pulled out.

What? "James?" I turned around. He was still standing there with a massive erection. Staring at me like he was analyzing something. "Did I do something wrong?"

"What? No." He grabbed my waist and lifted me onto the edge of the bed. He gently kissed my lips. "I just don't want to look back on this and regret not making love to you on our first Christmas together. Because I love you, Penny. With everything that I am. I loved your present, but..."

"Make love to me, James." He was scorching hot. And had the most brilliant mind. But he was kind and sweet too. And in that moment, I loved that side of him. I wanted to make love with him too. I had never been in love with someone during Christmas. I wanted to savor this moment forever.

He kissed me again and entered me slowly. Almost painfully slowly. I spread my thighs wider.

His kisses trailed down the side of my neck as he unhooked my corset. He peeled it off and kissed down the front of my chest and my right breast.

"James," I cried as his tongue slowly circled my nipple.

"I love you." He kissed between my breasts. "I love you." He kissed my other breast.

I hitched my legs around his waist.

He groaned.

I grabbed his face and brought his lips back to mine.

He started to move his hips faster. Making me climb higher and higher. I buried my fingers in his hair, not knowing how else to show him how much I loved this.

He groaned again and I exploded into a million pieces. I felt his warmth spread into me again and again.

With all the Christmas cards and Christmas presents I had gotten in my entire life, nothing made my heart feel warmer than this gift. His love.

"James," I panted.

He smiled down at me and brushed a strand of hair out of my face. "Penny."

"I need to tell you something important. Wherever you are...that's home to me. You're home to me."

His smile grew. "You saw my note to Santa."

"Yes. But it doesn't make what I said any less true. I was actually thinking that exact same thing last night when we were ice skating. New York feels like home to me. And it's because of you. I love you so much."

He slowly pulled out of me. "That truly was all that I wanted."

"I know. But I got you a few other things too." I climbed off the bed and started taking off the rest of my costume so I could put on pajamas.

"You can keep the garter on," James said. "I might want a second round."

I turned toward him. His hair was mussed up in that just-after-sex way. He had pulled on a pair of pajama bottoms with pictures of Santa hats all over them that I had set out for him last night. He looked adorable and sexy at the same time. How could I say no to that? I grabbed one of my silky robes and tied it around my waist.

"Deal," I said. "As long as round two is underneath the tree."

He smiled. "Deal."

I grabbed his hand. "Let's go see what Santa brought us!"

He laughed as I pulled him toward the hall.

When I stepped out of our bedroom I froze. There was garland on the staircase. And little red twinkle lights. I took a few steps down so that I could see into the living room. There were decorations everywhere. And not just random Christmassy things thrown around. They were very elaborate decorations. I slowly walked down the stairs as if I was in a trance. The Christmas tree had more ornaments and it even possessed a tree skirt now. More garland hung around the room and it looked like it had been sprinkled with the snow falling outside. There was even fake snow in front of the fireplace with boot prints to make it look like Santa had come down the chimney. Which was impossible. Because our fireplace was electric and we had no chimney.

There was no music. But *Believe* by Josh Groban started playing in my head. It was like I had just stepped into a fairytale. A perfect Christmas fairytale. How had James done all this? He must have been up all night. I was supposed to be Santa. But James had completely outdone me. Our once scarcely decorated apartment was now officially a Christmas wonderland. I turned toward him. "Oh my God."

"I know. Santa must have stopped in our apartment for quite awhile."

I laughed. "James, this is the best present anyone has ever gotten me. Thank you."

"I didn't do it."

I hit his arm playfully. "Show me everything." I couldn't help but twirl around. The Christmas music was still playing in my head.

He looked around like he was examining everything too. "It wasn't me, Penny."

"Of course it was you. Who else would it be?"

"I'm telling you, it must have been Santa." He pointed to the fireplace. "Look, he even left boot prints."

I smiled at him. "He also left us a red table-cloth on the dining room table. And gold placemats. He has an eye for interior design."

James shrugged. "I guess he does."

"James, just admit that you did this. I know it was you. And I love it so much. Here I thought you were a Grinch and then you did all this. It's magical in here."

"It wasn't me," he insisted.

I laughed. "I wonder what he left in our stockings," I said. I grabbed them off the hooks and handed him his.

"Huh," James said. "It appears he did leave us gifts." He lifted out the bags of his favorite chocolates. He pressed his lips together.

"Oh my God," I said. "My favorite choco-lates." I pulled out the bag of chocolate that I had put in my own stocking.

"Did you do this?" he asked.

"No. Did you?" I gestured to the completely transformed apartment.

The corner of his mouth lifted slightly. "No," he said defensively.

I knew he was lying. And I was pretty sure he knew I was lying. But we both stayed silent. We both wanted to give each other the magic of Christmas. That was the sweetest gift anyone had ever given me.

"This really wasn't you?" he asked and gestured to the stocking.

"No," I lied. "And it wasn't you?"

"Nope."

"So either a crazy Christmas lover broke into our apartment, or Santa Claus is real." Saying it out loud sounded insane. But what if it really hadn't been James? What if Santa did exist? I shook the thought away.

"Both those options sound crazy." But I saw his eyes gravitate toward his stocking again.

Suddenly I realized that it didn't just look like Christmas. It smelled like Christmas too. "What's that smell?"

James shrugged. "I have no idea. It smells kind of like spaghetti."

Spaghetti? *Oh my God.* I ran into the kitchen. There was a lasagna assembled on the kitchen counter. My mom always made lasagna on Christmas. I had told James that a few weeks ago.

James came up behind me and kissed the back of my neck.

"Why won't you just admit that you did all this?" I couldn't seem to stop smiling. This was hands down the most wonderful gift I had ever received.

"Because I didn't." He lifted up the note that was lying next to the pan. We both looked down at it.

Dear Penny and James,

May the love that you share grow and grow and put smiles on your faces every day of the year. Take the joy from one day and spread it to all of them. That's the true spirit of Christmas.

-S

P.S. Put the lasagna in the oven for 35 minutes at 375 degrees.

It wasn't James' handwriting. I stared at the note.

"See, it wasn't me," he said again. "S probably stands for Santa."

I laughed. "Santa made us lasagna?"

He shrugged. "He seems like a talented guy."

"Mhm." I wrapped my arms around him. "All of this must have taken all night. I just hope he can see how appreciative I am."

"Well...if he sees you while you're sleeping..."

I laughed and pressed my face against his chest. I wasn't even sure if the smell of Christmas was my favorite smell anymore. I'm pretty sure it was James' cologne.

A knock on the door made James groan. "It's so early," he said. "We haven't even had time for round two."

"I think it's sweet that they came so early. It means they want to spend time with us on Christmas."

"Go answer the door. I'll put the lasagna in."

"For breakfast?"

"New tradition," he said with a laugh.

Actually, I was kind of in the mood for breakfast lasagna. These new traditions were pretty wonderful. I opened up the door. Mason, Matt, and Rob, were all standing there with huge smiles on their faces and presents in their arms.

"Merry Christmas!" Mason said and gave me a hug. "Thanks for inviting us." He placed a kiss on my cheek and went to put the presents under the tree.

Matt hugged me and lifted me off my feet slightly. "Merry Christmas," he said before setting me back down on my feet. "Last night was my favorite anti-Christmas ever."

I laughed as I watched him join Mason by the tree.

"Looks like a few little elves were busy in here last night," Rob said. "It looks great."

He didn't say it, but the way he was looking around made me think that he had helped.

"Did you help James with this?" I asked.

"James? Psh. No. This was clearly the work of Santa. James is a Grinch, remember? And I most certainly had nothing to do with this. It's a little over the top if you ask me."

I laughed. *Yup, he definitely helped.* "You know, I thought James was a Grinch too. But I'm not so sure anymore." No one that spent the time to do all this was a Grinch. I turned to see James coming toward us.

"Do you want some help with that?" James asked and reached for the present Rob was holding.

Rob awkwardly jerked away. "No. It's not for you."

"I can still put it under the tree," James said and reached for it again.

Rob took another step back.

I was pretty sure I noticed the precarious placement of the present at the exact same time as James.

"If your dick is in that box and you're planning on giving it to Penny, I will knock you out."

Rob's eyes bulged. "What? I'm not going to dick-in-the-box her."

"Then give me the present," James said and reached for it again.

"I need to use the restroom!" Rob said and started to walk down the hall. Right before he entered the bathroom he turned around and let go of the box that was positioned in front of his waist. The box didn't move. "It's my dick in a box!" he sang.

I started laughing hysterically.

James stepped toward him, but Rob had already gone into the bathroom and slammed the door. James turned back to me. Soon enough he was laughing too.

By the time Rob came back out of the bathroom, we were all sitting by the tree with huge smiles on our faces. I took a look around at all the new people in my life. This group of friends that had adopted me as one of their own. And I felt so loved.

It didn't matter what was under the tree. James had already given me the greatest gift. And the fact that he was wondering about where the presents in the stockings came from gave me hope that maybe a small part of him believed too. All the Christmas music and movies and decorations in the world didn't compare to this feeling at all. The warmth in my chest wanted to bubble over to tears. But I didn't want anyone to mistake my happy tears for sad ones.

"I'm going to go check on the lasagna," I said and excused myself from the group. I took a deep breath when I entered the kitchen and looked out the window. The snow was falling, blanketing the city in white. It was like the whole city stood still for Christmas.

"Merry Christmas, baby," James said and wrapped his arm around my back as he joined me by the window.

"Merry Christmas, James." I smiled up at him.

"I need to tell you something important."

It was the same thing I had said to him earlier. When I told him he was home to me. I was pretty sure he was going to confess to reading my note to Santa. "And what is that?" I turned away from the snow to give him my undivided attention. Because despite the magic of a Christmas snow, I was enjoying what was right in front of me more. I stared into his brown eyes.

"When I was little, I loved Christmas. But for the past several years, Christmas was just another day. And honestly, I was relieved when it was over." He tucked a loose strand of hair behind my ear. "Maybe I had turned into a little bit of a Grinch."

"Just a little." I bit the inside of my lip so I wouldn't smile too hard.

"Now everything's changed. No day with you is just another day. Every day seems better than the last. And I think I forgot how magical Christmas could be until I met you. So thank you. For reminding me."

"I hope that every Christmas is as wonderful as this one," I said as I wrapped my arms behind his neck.

"It just gets better from here, baby."

"How did Santa know?" I said and looked up at the ceiling. A sprig of mistletoe was hung directly above us.

"Like I said earlier. He's a pretty talented guy." James' lips brushed against mine. I stood on my tiptoes to deepen the kiss.

Santa was definitely talented. And for just a second, I let myself believe that maybe James really hadn't decorated our apartment. Maybe Santa really did exist. I never wanted to lose the Christmas spirit. And as long as I had James, I knew I'd never become a Grinch.

What's Next?

Want more of James and Penny? Then go read Obsessed! It's the story of how he met Penny told from his point-of-view.

I'm not a good man. And it turns out I'm an even worse professor.

I have sinful thoughts about one of my students. Every night. I picture her in my bed. In my shower. Underneath me. Right up against the chalkboard. I'm especially fond of that one.

In my defense, I know her thoughts are as sinful as mine. She's begging me with her beautiful blue eyes. She's daring me to cross the line.

Get your copy today!

The Tutor

James and Penny aren't the only couple who got down and dirty at New Castle University. Just ask Sophia… She gets crazy right on campus!

Sophia has had a crush on Wyatt ever since they met. Tutoring him at the library once a week has been the highlight of her semester. But their sexual tension is slowly torturing her. Wyatt is sexy, funny, flirtatious, and as far as she can tell - completely unattainable.

When it is time for their last tutoring session, she worries it will be the last time she will ever get to see him. She's determined to not let that happen. Dreaming about him and watching him from a distance at his baseball games isn't going to cut it.
But will she have the confidence to confess her true feelings?

For your free copy, go to:
www.ivysmoak.com/the-tutor-freebie

About the Author

Ivy Smoak is the Wall Street Journal, USA Today, and Amazon #1 bestselling author of *The Hunted Series*. Her books have sold over 2 million copies worldwide.

When she's not writing, you can find Ivy binge watching too many TV shows, taking long walks, playing outside, and generally refusing to act like an adult. She lives with her husband in Delaware.

Facebook: IvySmoakAuthor
Instagram: @IvySmoakAuthor
Goodreads: IvySmoak

Printed in Great Britain
by Amazon

82751839R00058